OPHELIA HOUSE

CRIMSON BLOSSOMS

ORIGINAL ARTWORK

ANDREW L. WILLIS

CREATED AND WRITTEN

CARLTON L. SAMPSON

COVER DESIGN, BALLOONS, PAGE LAYOUT

Palanquin

MAITRESSE DORMITORY
SIN PO ACADEMY
BRYN MAWR

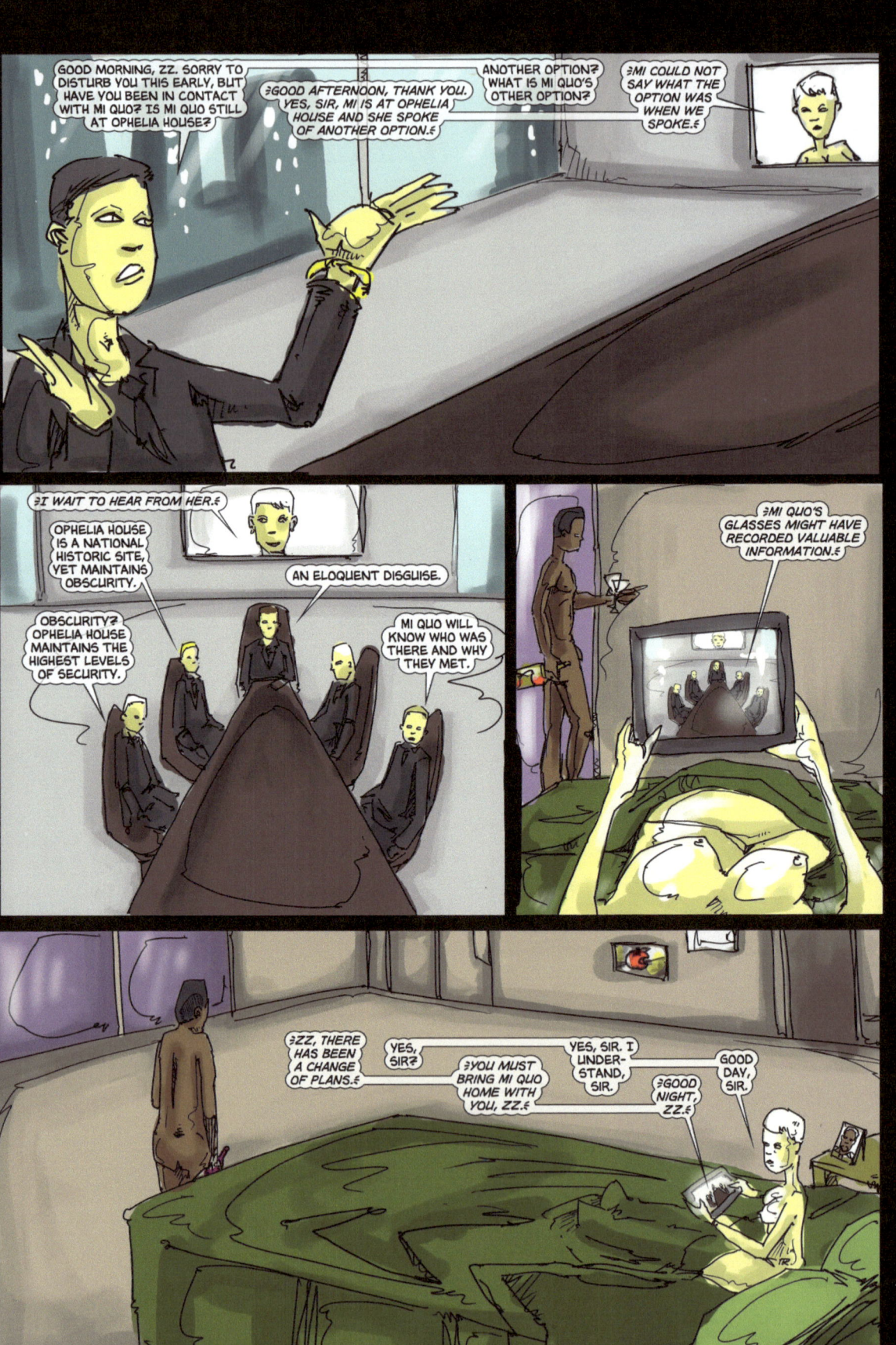

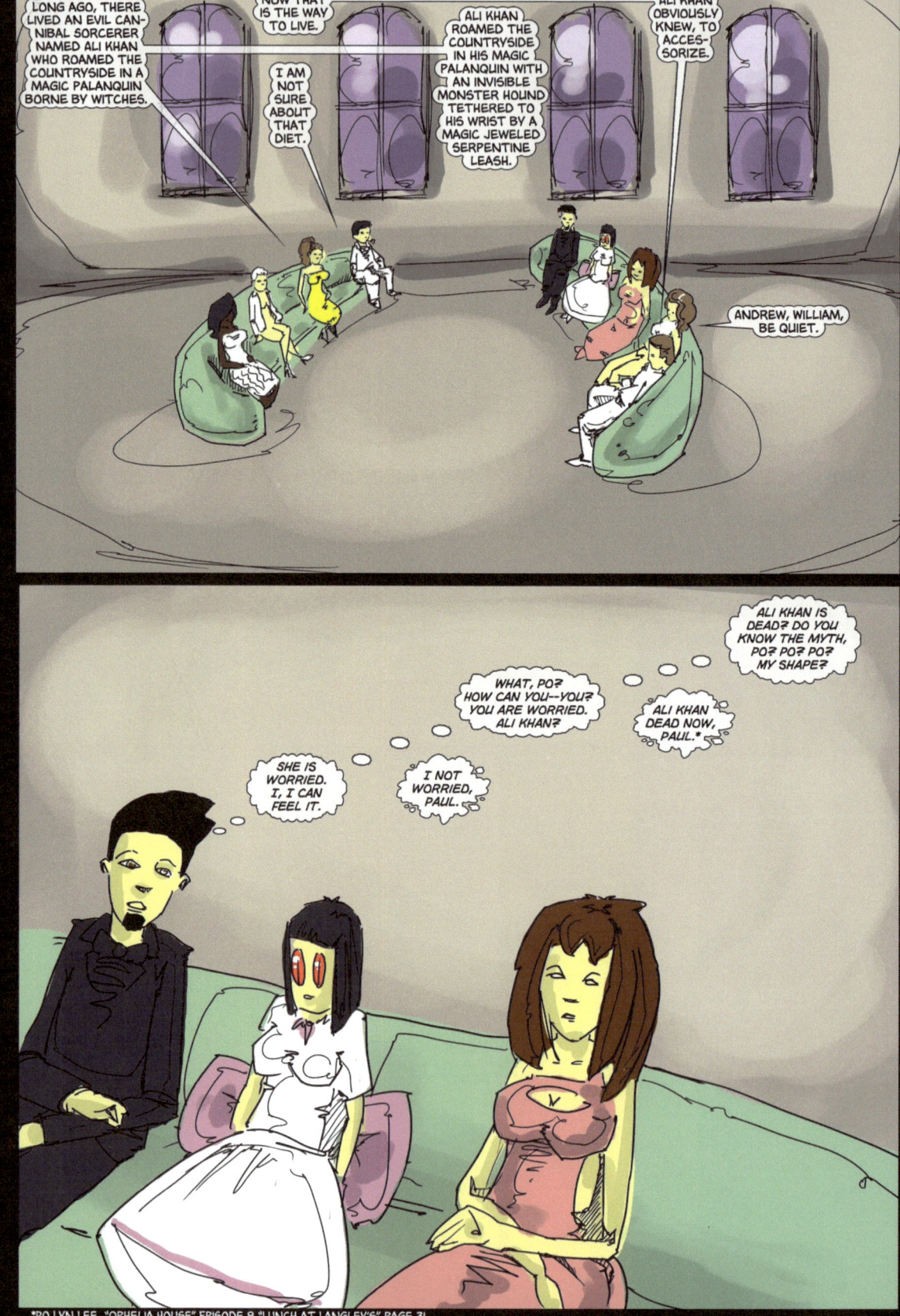

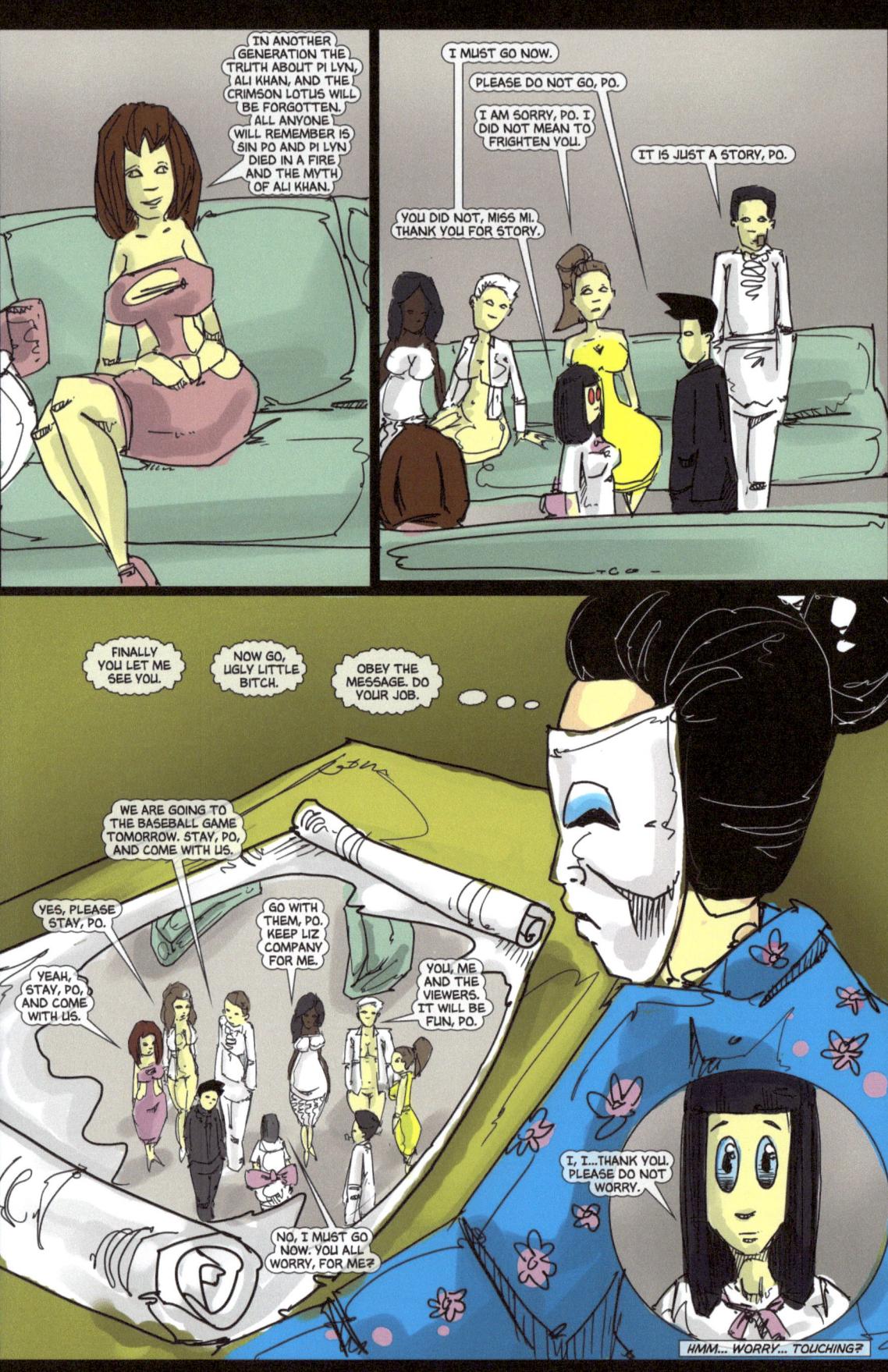

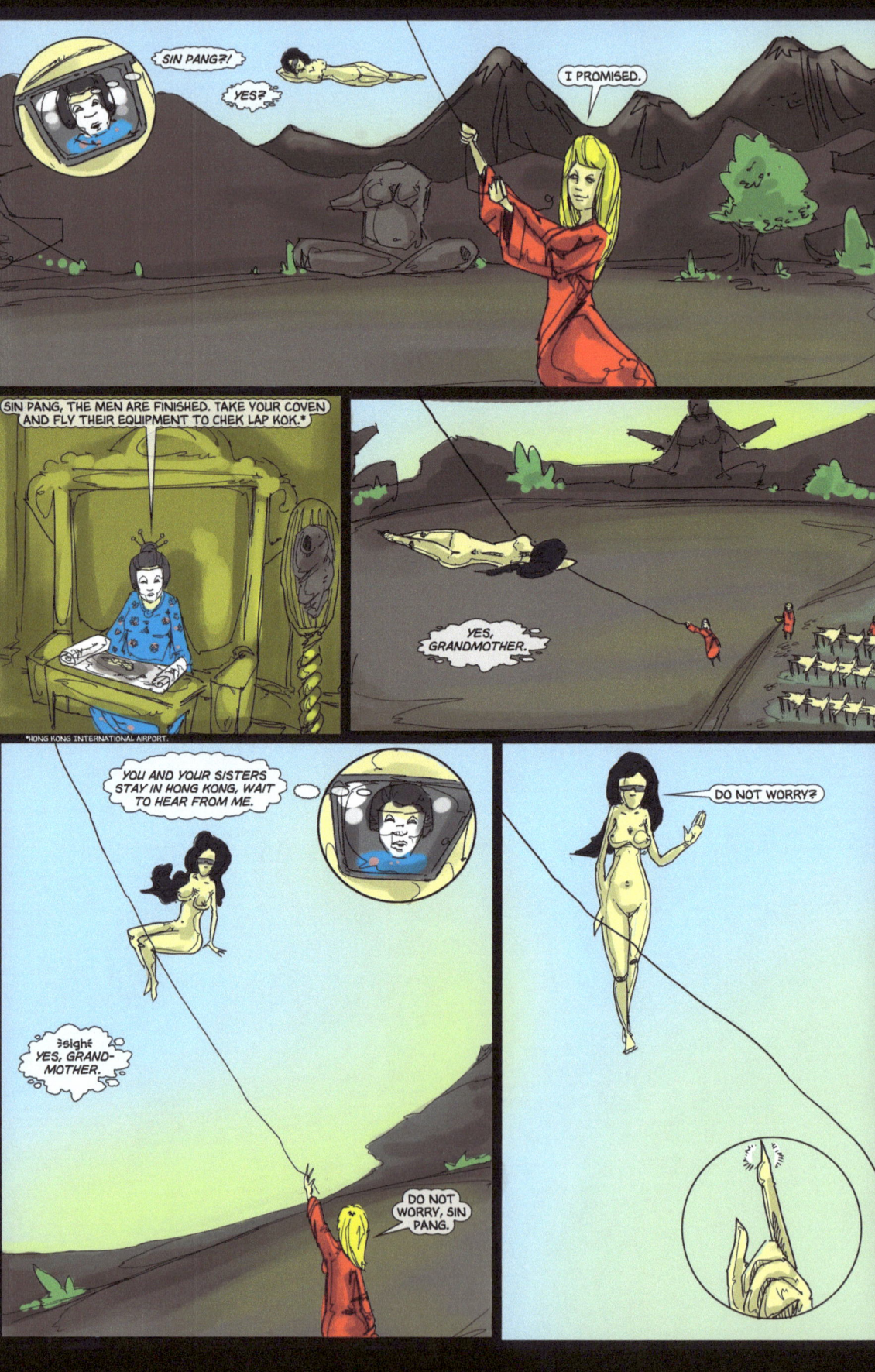

*HONG KONG INTERNATIONAL AIRPORT.

SIN PO ACADEMY BRYN MAWR, MAITRESSE DORMITORY, SUNDAY, 3:41 AM EASTERN STANDARD TIME
SHE HAS SEEN THE PARCHMENT. SHE WEARS THE BOND. CALL UPON THE SIRYN. WAKE THE SIRYN TO DEVOUR HER.
Yes, Grandmother.
Grandmother, Quan's bond gnaws.
QUAN HAS DISOBEYED ME. HE WILL BE PUNISHED. A NEW MALE MUST WEAR THE BOND FOR YOUR BROOD.
squahiss
squahiss
squahiss
squahiss
QUAN HAS A DRIVER, FABIO. SOON WE WILL BOND WITH FABIO. SEE THAT FABIO IS PREPARED.
squahiss
squahiss
squahiss
IKIRU, I HEAR IT IN MARTHA'S SCROLL. IT IS SHADOWED BY MARTHA'S BOND. IT IS NEAR. IT MUST BE TONIGHT, IKIRU. IT KNOWS QUAN HAS SEEN IT.
Yes, Grandmother.
I UNDERSTAND, GRAND MOTHER.
squahiss

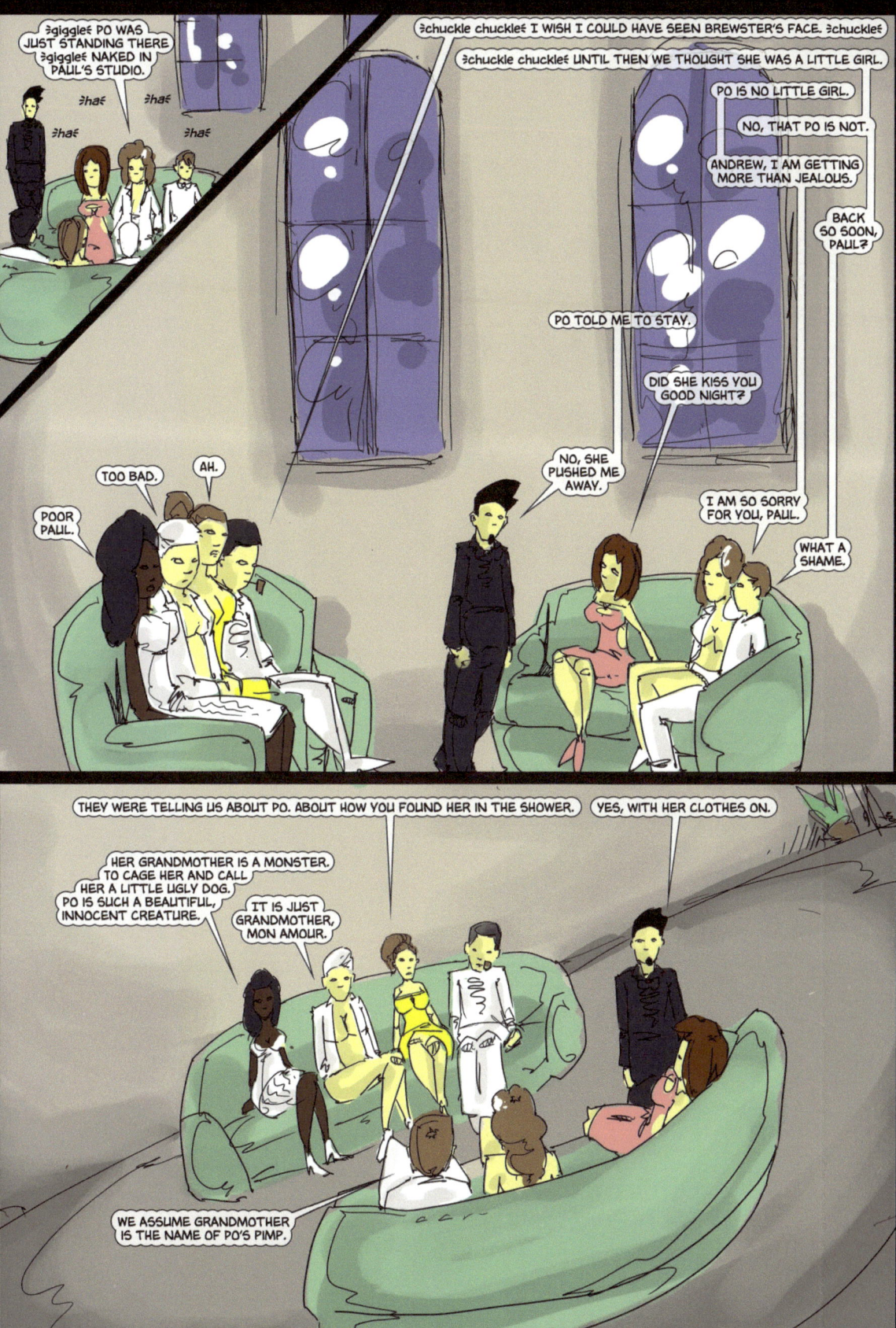

HOW DID PO GET IN YOUR APARTMENT?
I HAD FRIENDS THERE PACKING. THEY MUST HAVE LET HER IN.
ARE YOU SURE? DID YOU ASK THEM?
NO, I JUST ASSUMED THEY HAD.
I CANNOT GET OVER THE FACT SOMEONE TOOK CARE OF YOU SOMEWHERE FOR THREE DAYS. WHY WERE YOU ATTACKED, PAUL? WAS IT A RANDOM ACT OF VIOLENCE?
sigh NO, I HAD DONE AN OIL OF THE THREE GUYS WHO ATTACKED ME DOING BUSINESS ON THE CORNER.
LET ME GUESS. YOU PUT THEM IN THE WINDOW?
I HAVE A STOREFRONT. THE PIECE, "LOCAL ECONOMIC EMPOWERMENT ZONE", SOLD IN THREE DAYS.
YOU DREW THEM TO YOU, PAUL.
ANDREW, STOP BEING SILLY.
BUT THAT WAS A GOOD ONE, GAIL.
ha ha
ha ha
ha ha
ha ha
YOU HAD A STOREFRONT. BREWSTER SOLD PAUL A STUDIO ON THE RIVER FOR TWO PAINTINGS AND ONE HUNDRED THOUSAND DOLLARS.
BREWSTER IS NO FOOL.
PERHAPS. chuckle BUT, BREWSTER KNOWS ART.
HELENA, WOULD YOU LIKE TO GO WITH ME TO RUPERT LA BELLE'S ART GALLERY TOMORROW? I WANT TO SEE THE PORNOGRAPHIC WALL HANGING OF ME AND WILLIAM.
REPETITIONS OF A RANDOM SHAPE, MI!

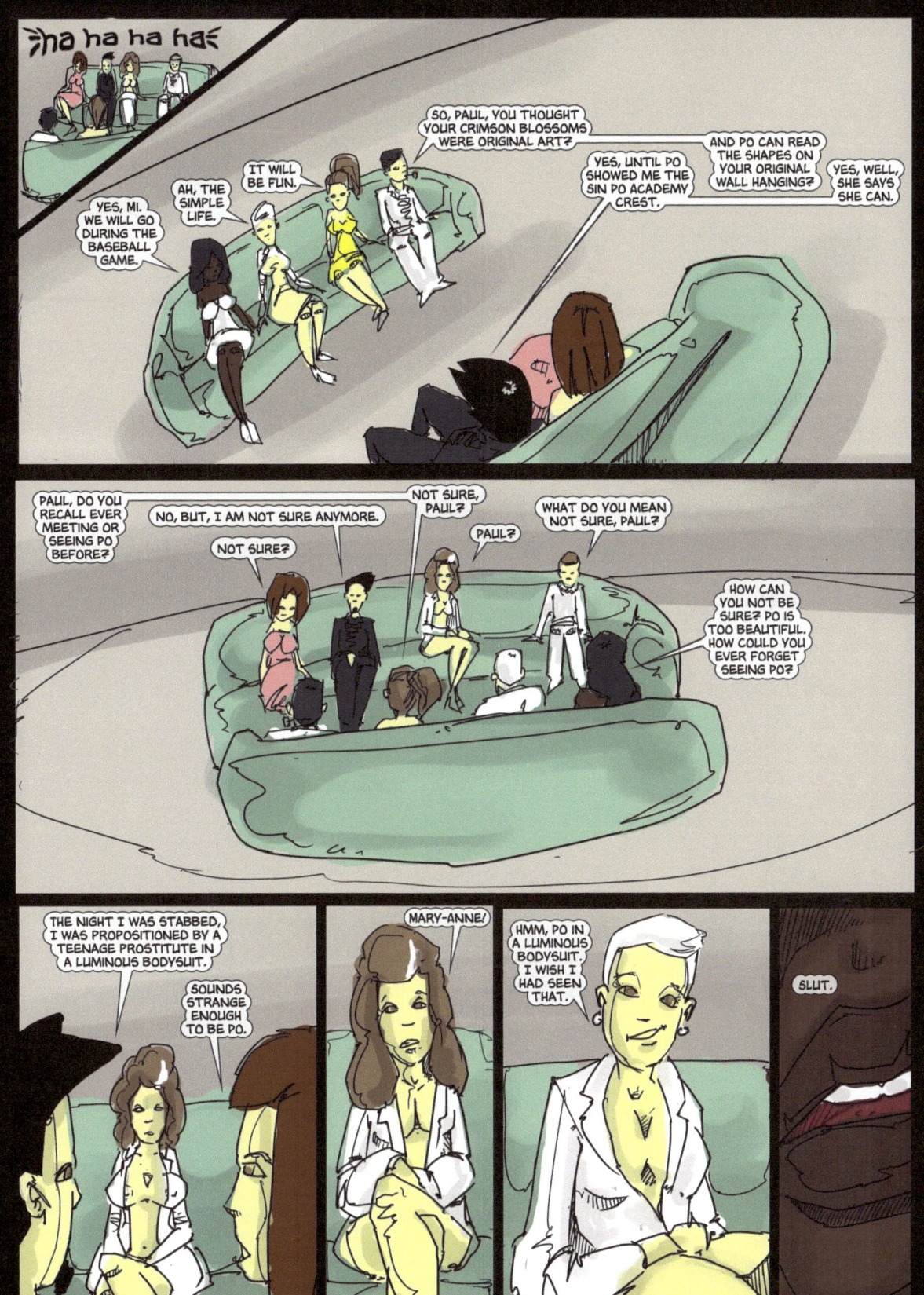

*PO LYN LEE "OPHELIA HOUSE" EPISODE 6 "ASSASSINS" PAGE 15

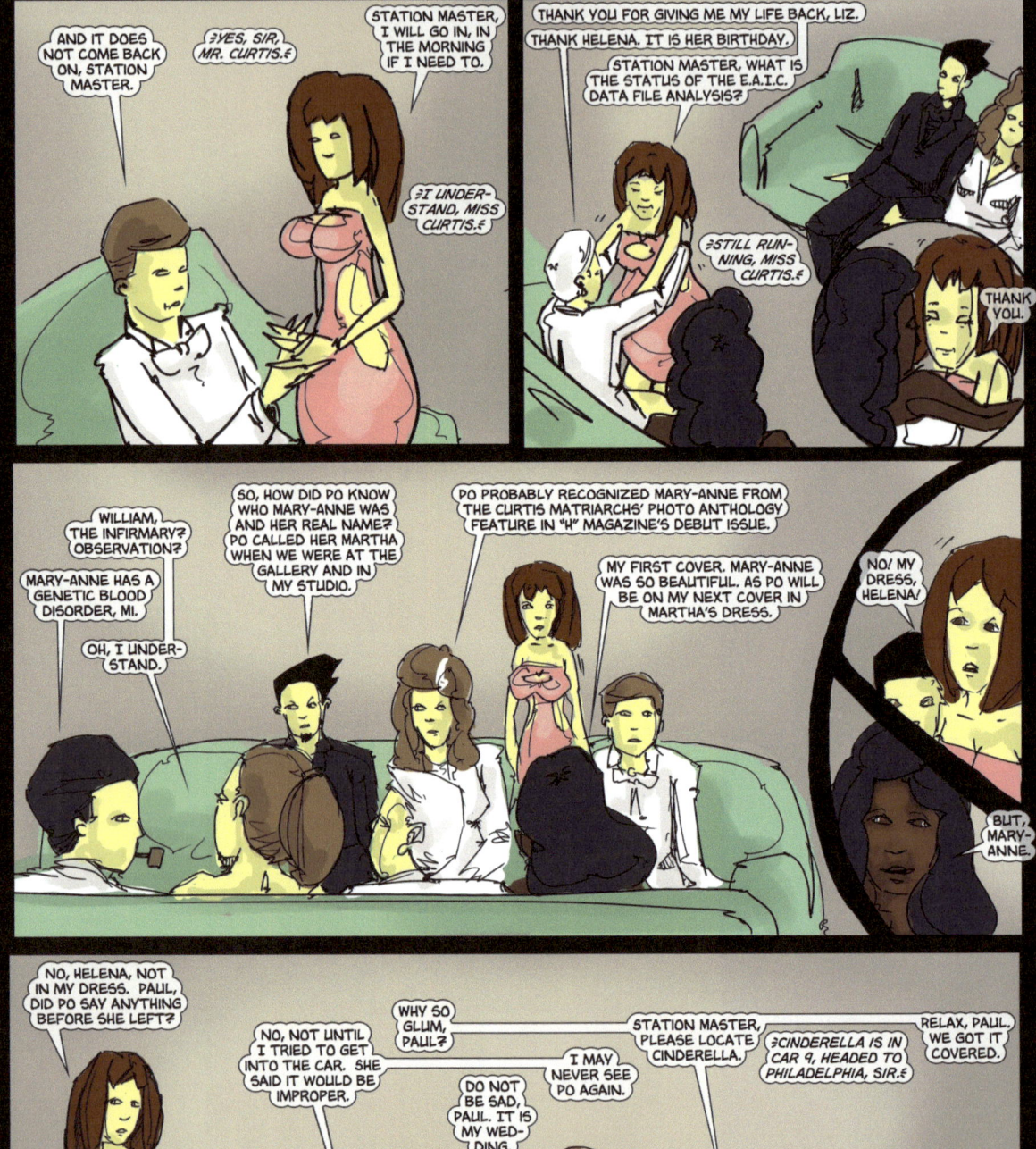

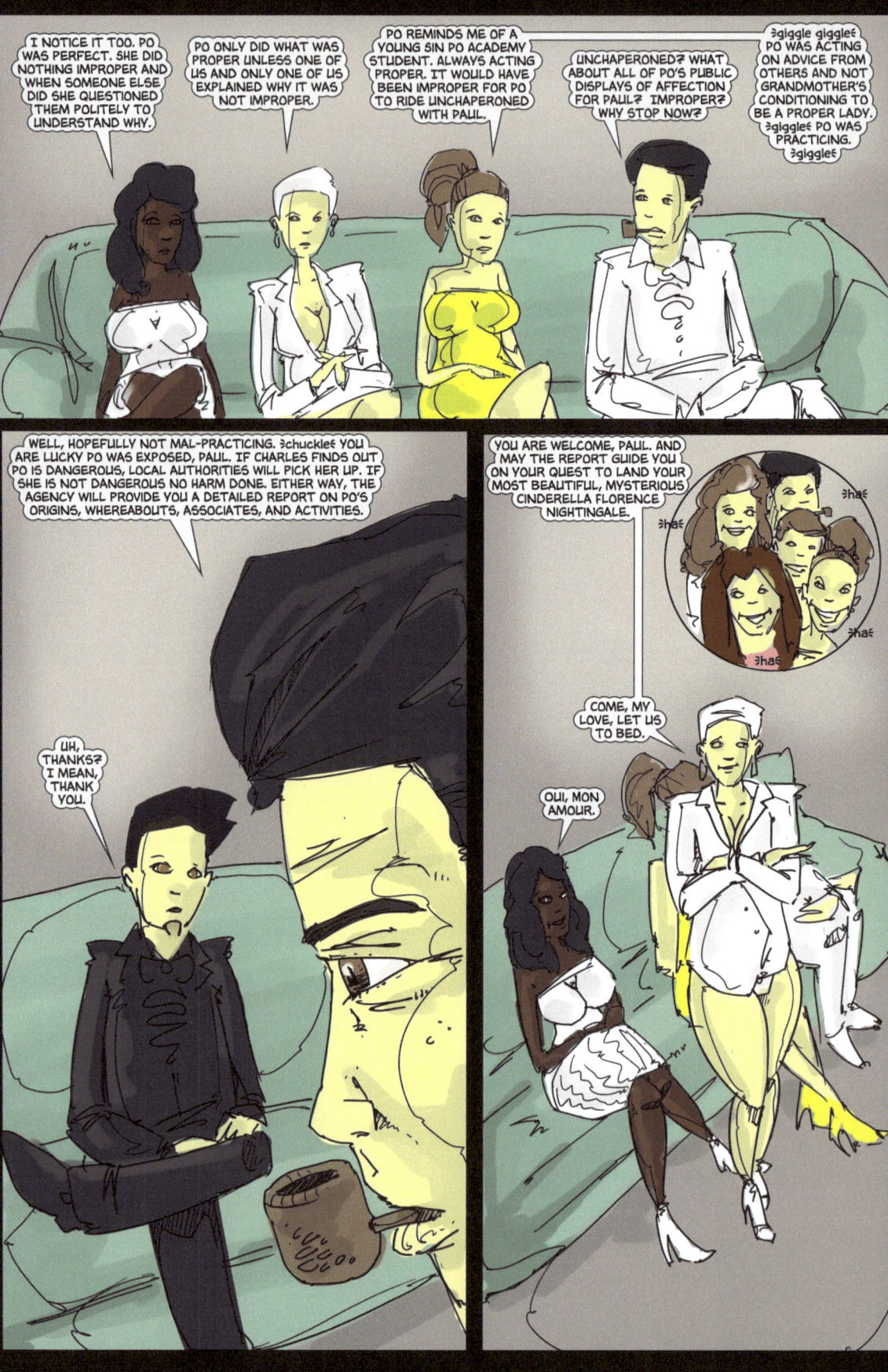

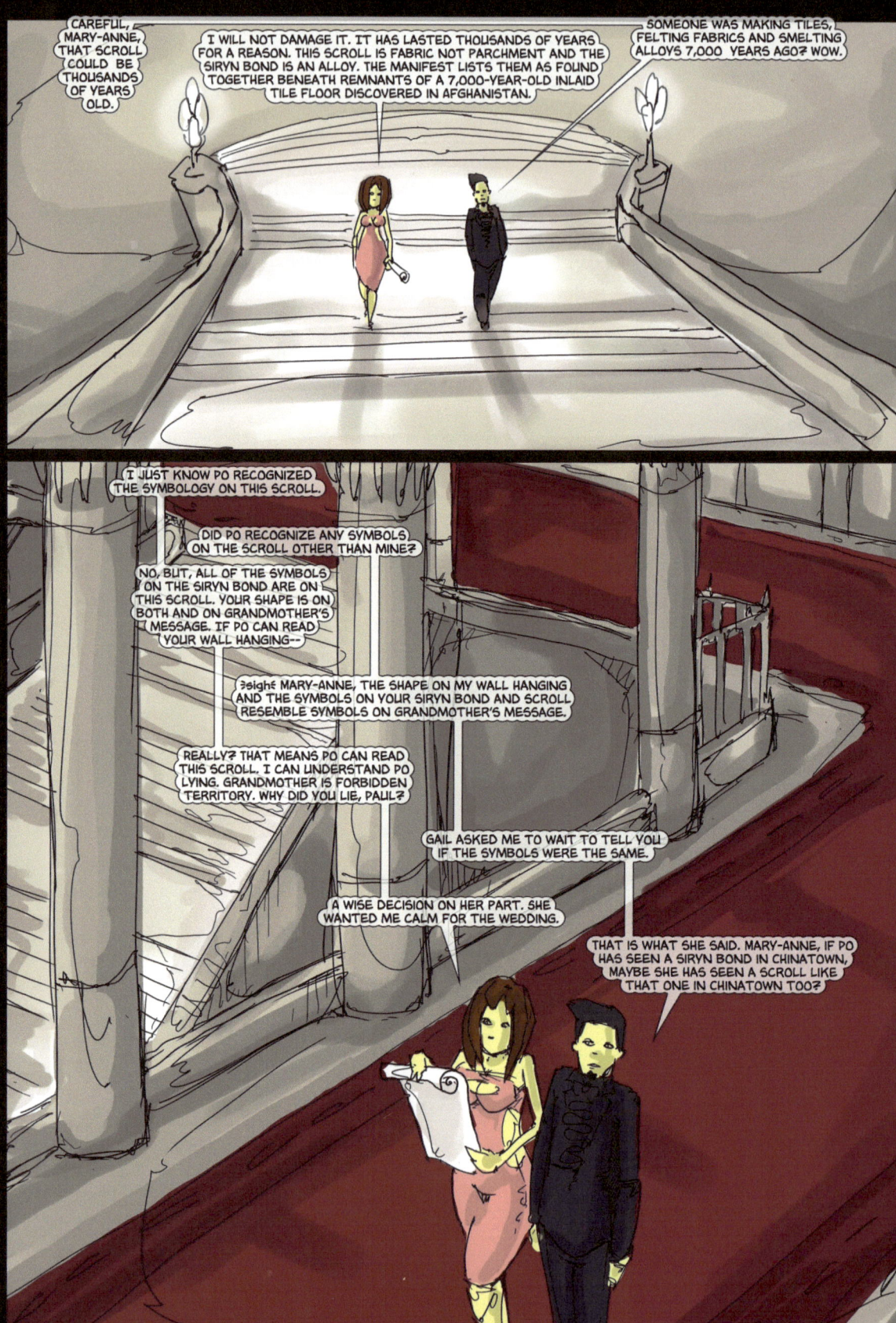

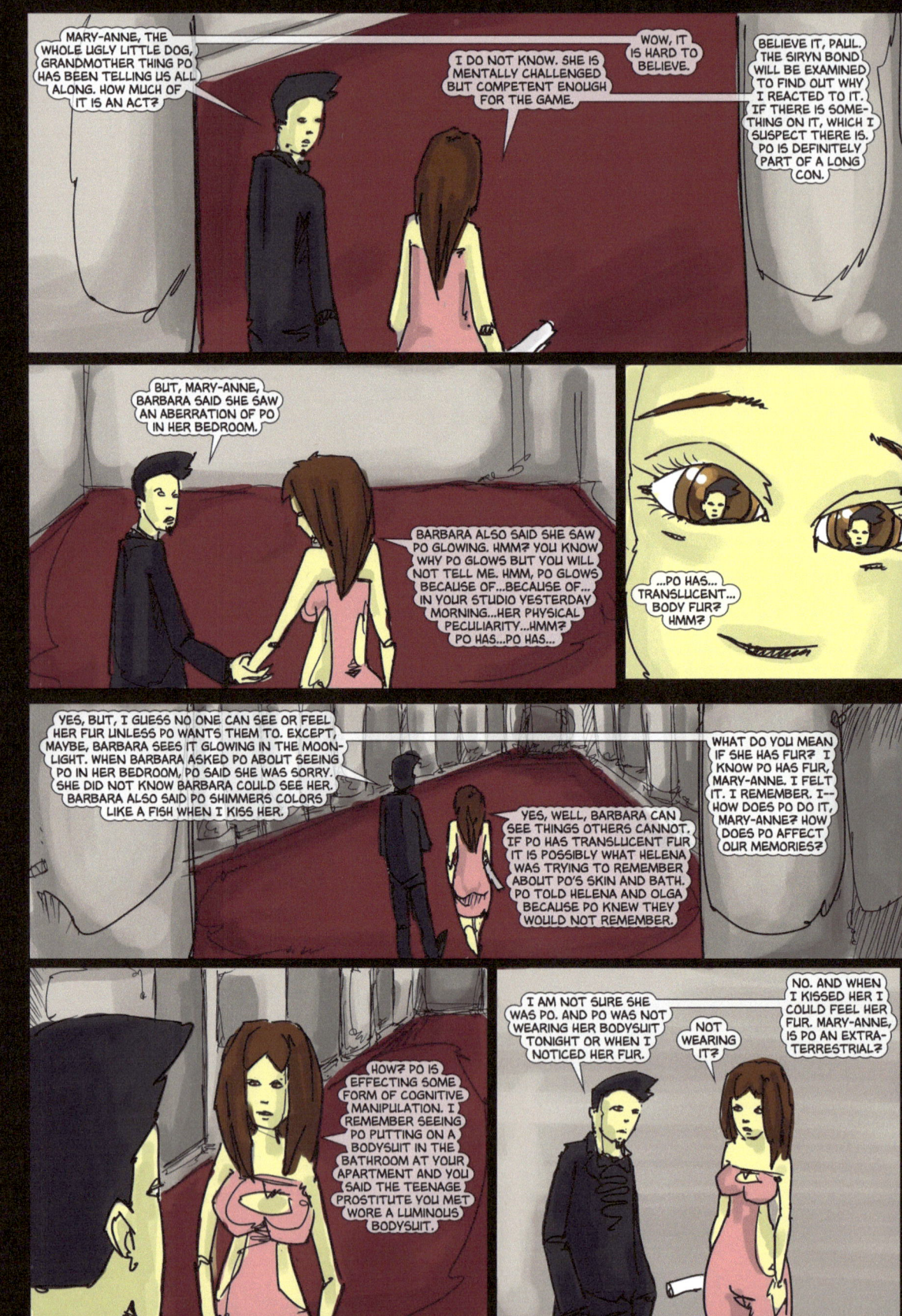

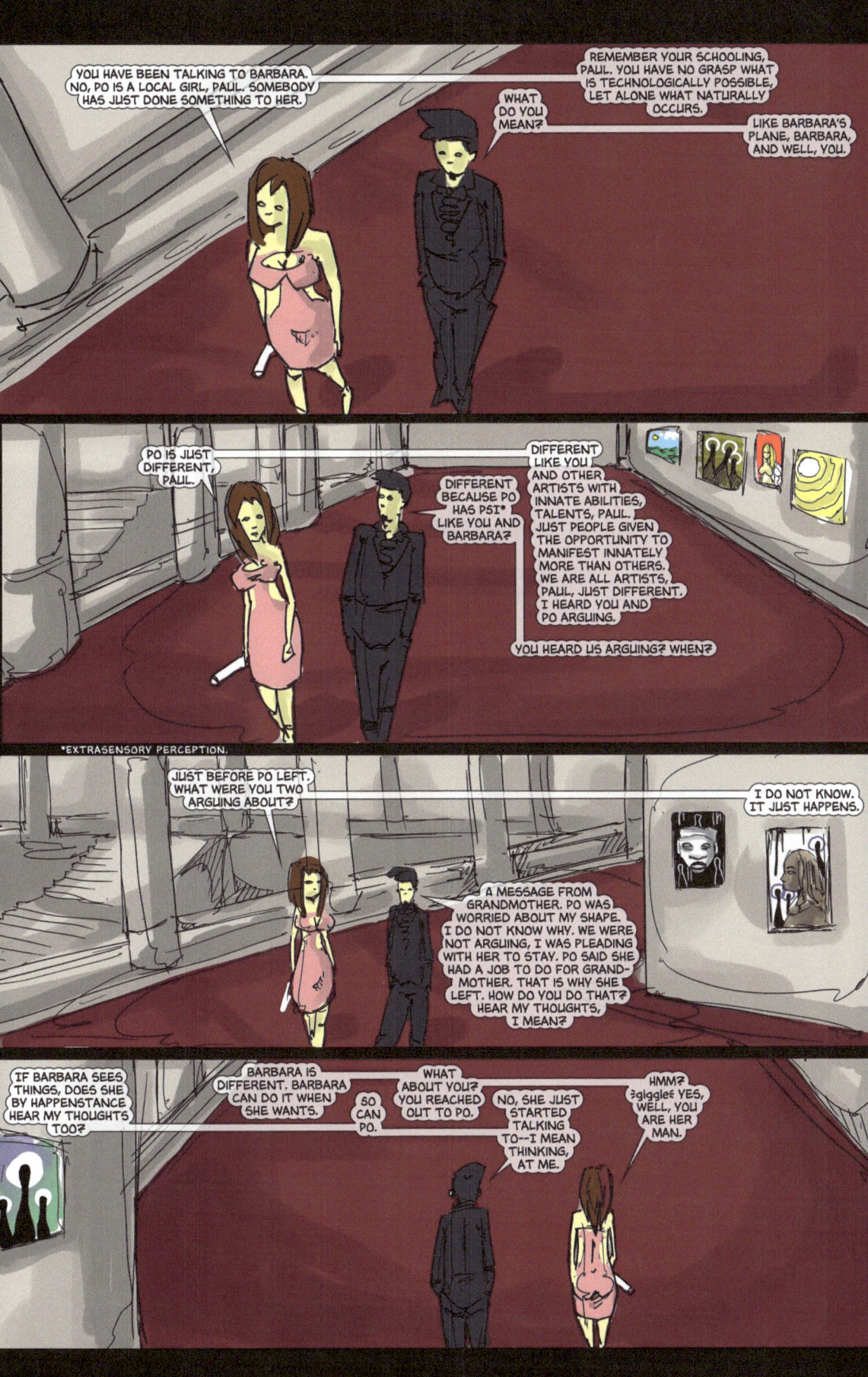

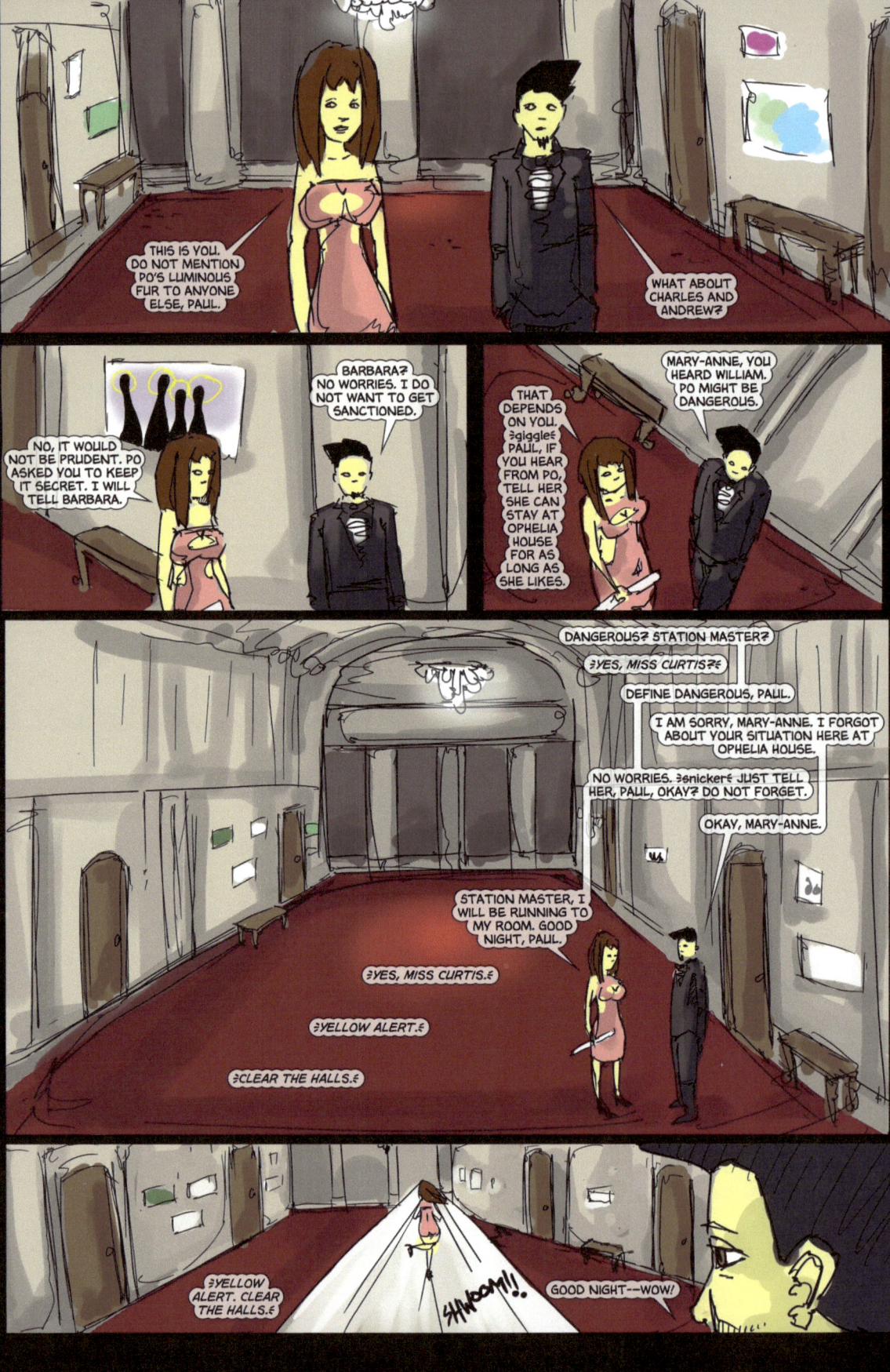

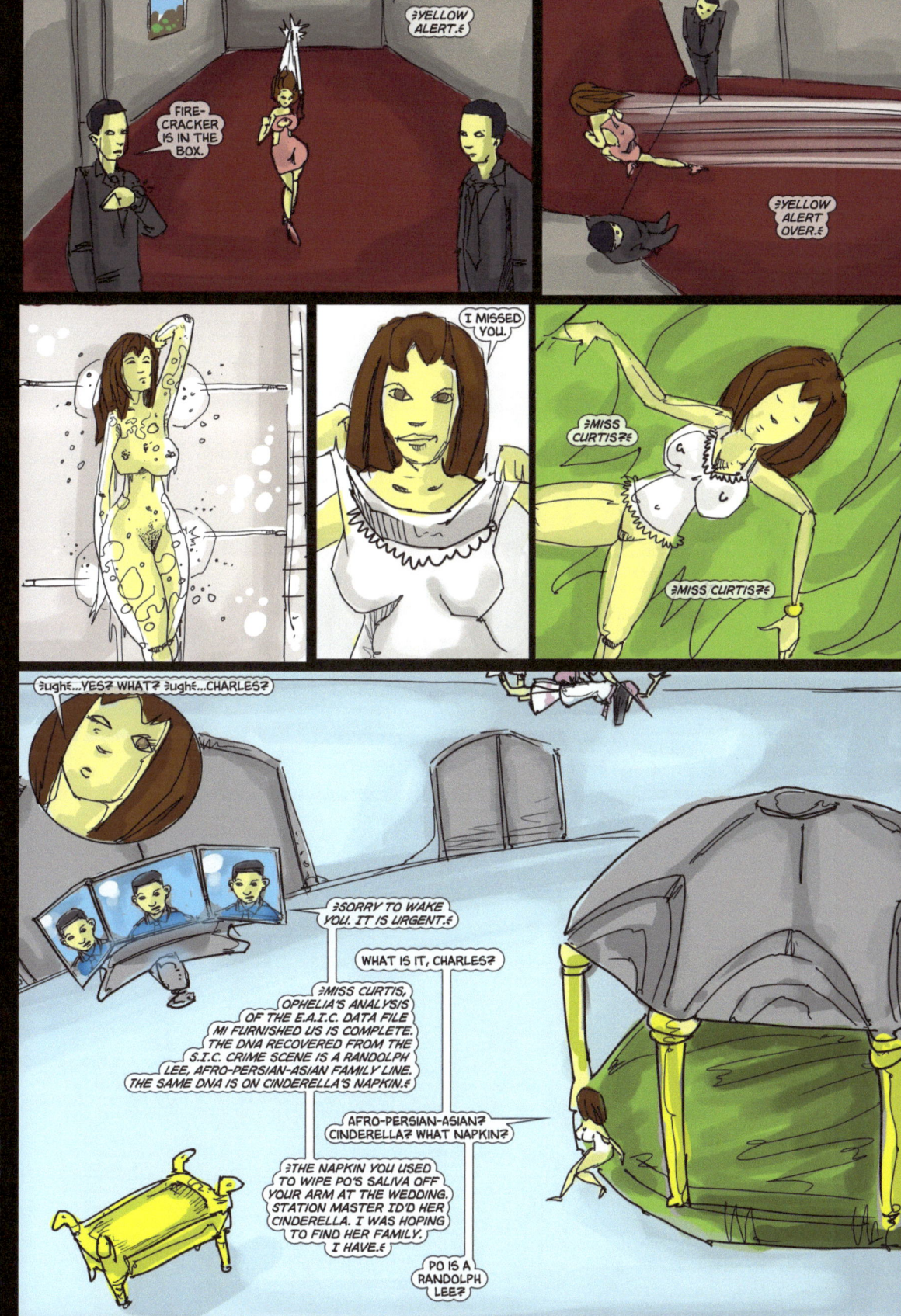

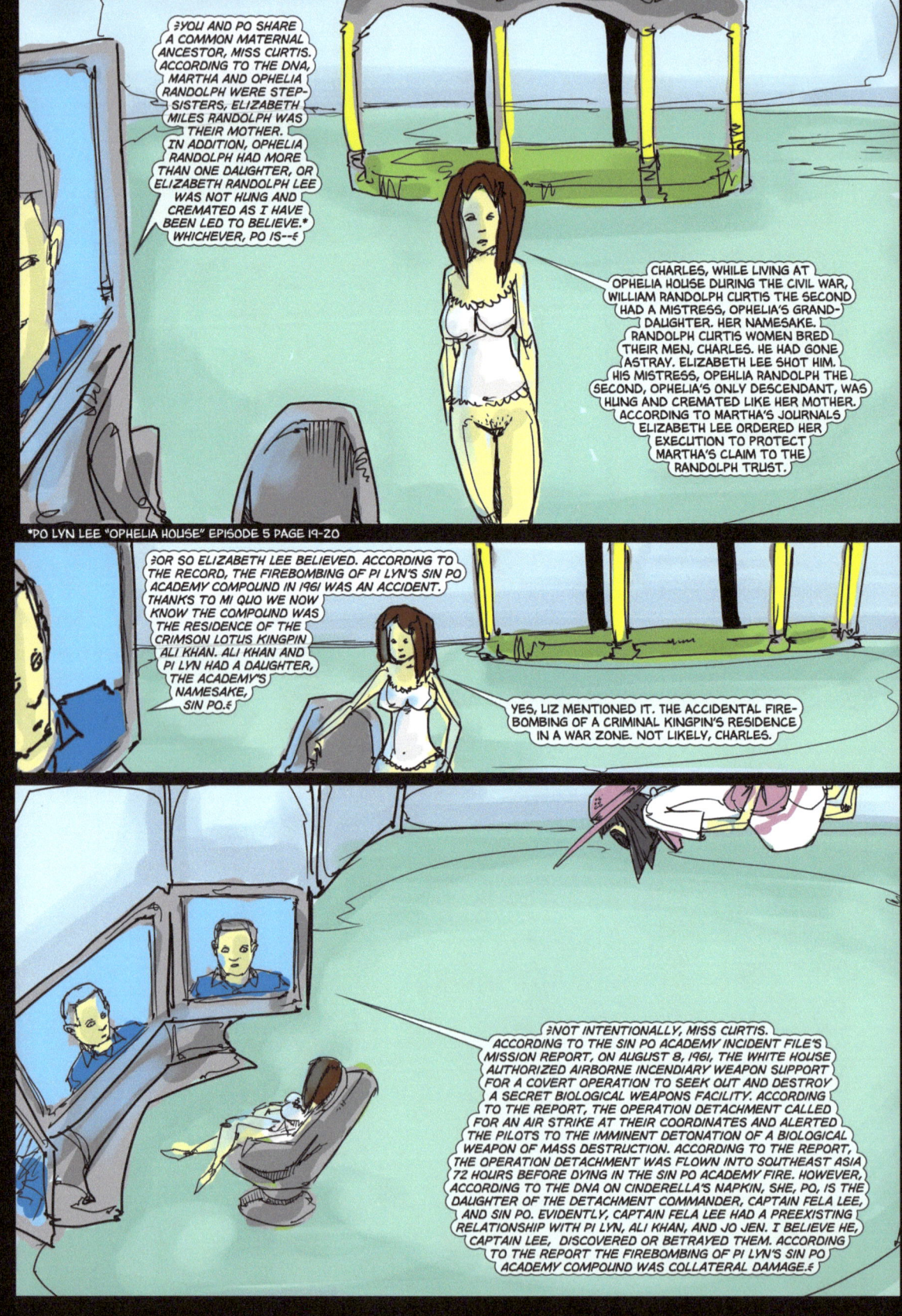

*PO LYN LEE "OPHELIA HOUSE" EPISODE 5 PAGE 19-20

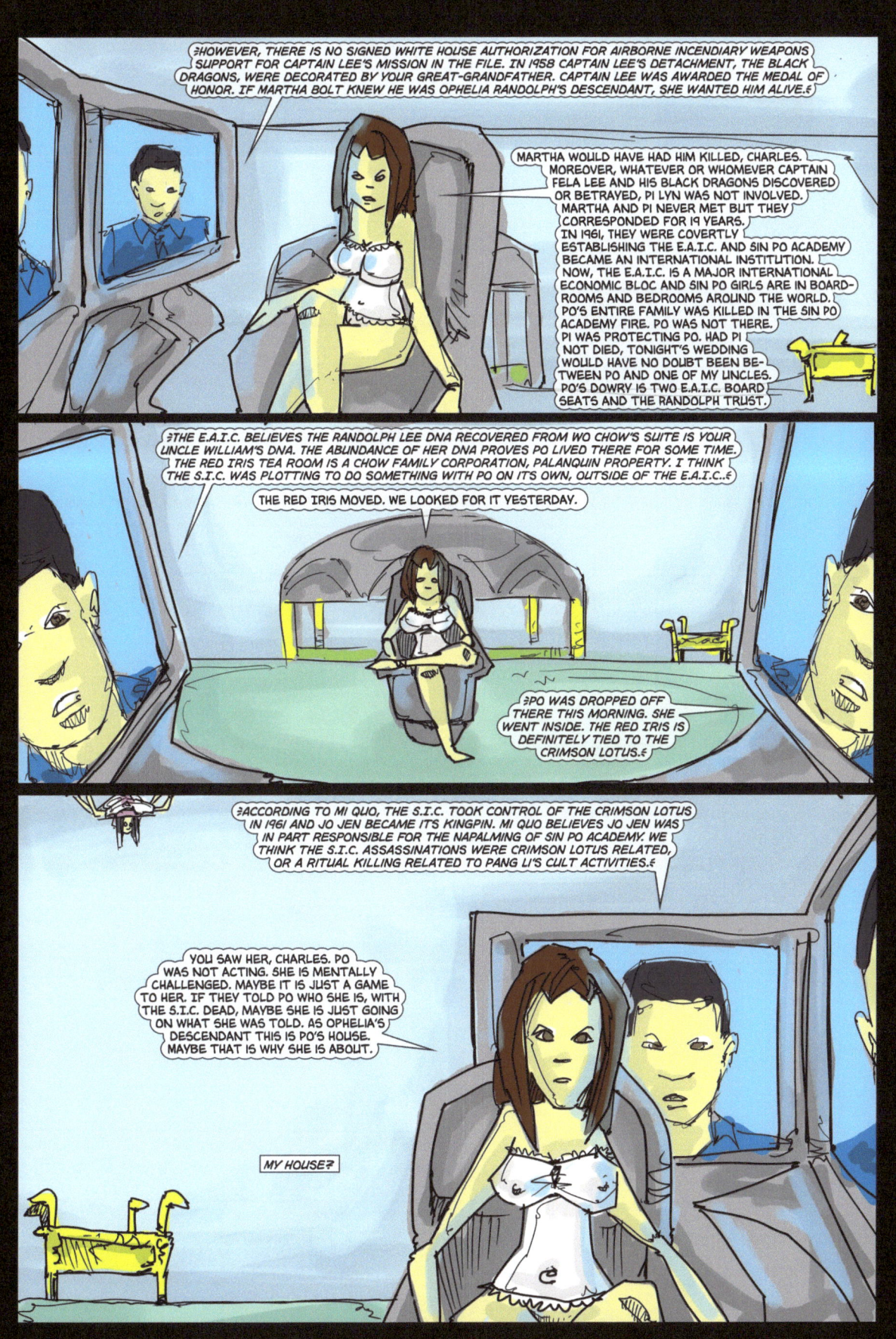

≥HOWEVER, THERE IS NO SIGNED WHITE HOUSE AUTHORIZATION FOR AIRBORNE INCENDIARY WEAPONS SUPPORT FOR CAPTAIN LEE'S MISSION IN THE FILE. IN 1958 CAPTAIN LEE'S DETACHMENT, THE BLACK DRAGONS, WERE DECORATED BY YOUR GREAT-GRANDFATHER. CAPTAIN LEE WAS AWARDED THE MEDAL OF HONOR. IF MARTHA BOLT KNEW HE WAS OPHELIA RANDOLPH'S DESCENDANT, SHE WANTED HIM ALIVE.≤

MARTHA WOULD HAVE HAD HIM KILLED, CHARLES. MOREOVER, WHATEVER OR WHOMEVER CAPTAIN FELA LEE AND HIS BLACK DRAGONS DISCOVERED OR BETRAYED, PI LYN WAS NOT INVOLVED. MARTHA AND PI NEVER MET BUT THEY CORRESPONDED FOR 19 YEARS. IN 1961, THEY WERE COVERTLY ESTABLISHING THE E.A.I.C. AND SIN PO ACADEMY BECAME AN INTERNATIONAL INSTITUTION. NOW, THE E.A.I.C. IS A MAJOR INTERNATIONAL ECONOMIC BLOC AND SIN PO GIRLS ARE IN BOARD-ROOMS AND BEDROOMS AROUND THE WORLD. PO'S ENTIRE FAMILY WAS KILLED IN THE SIN PO ACADEMY FIRE. PO WAS NOT THERE. PI WAS PROTECTING PO. HAD PI NOT DIED, TONIGHT'S WEDDING WOULD HAVE NO DOUBT BEEN BE-TWEEN PO AND ONE OF MY UNCLES. PO'S DOWRY IS TWO E.A.I.C. BOARD SEATS AND THE RANDOLPH TRUST.

≥THE E.A.I.C. BELIEVES THE RANDOLPH LEE DNA RECOVERED FROM WO CHOW'S SUITE IS YOUR UNCLE WILLIAM'S DNA. THE ABUNDANCE OF HER DNA PROVES PO LIVED THERE FOR SOME TIME. THE RED IRIS TEA ROOM IS A CHOW FAMILY CORPORATION, PALANQUIN PROPERTY. I THINK THE S.I.C. WAS PLOTTING TO DO SOMETHING WITH PO ON ITS OWN, OUTSIDE OF THE E.A.I.C..≤

THE RED IRIS MOVED. WE LOOKED FOR IT YESTERDAY.

≥PO WAS DROPPED OFF THERE THIS MORNING. SHE WENT INSIDE. THE RED IRIS IS DEFINITELY TIED TO THE CRIMSON LOTUS.≤

≥ACCORDING TO MI QUO, THE S.I.C. TOOK CONTROL OF THE CRIMSON LOTUS IN 1961 AND JO JEN BECAME ITS KINGPIN. MI QUO BELIEVES JO JEN IS IN PART RESPONSIBLE FOR THE NAPALMING OF SIN PO ACADEMY. WE THINK THE S.I.C. ASSASSINATIONS WERE CRIMSON LOTUS RELATED, OR A RITUAL KILLING RELATED TO PANG LI'S CULT ACTIVITIES.≤

YOU SAW HER, CHARLES. PO WAS NOT ACTING. SHE IS MENTALLY CHALLENGED. MAYBE IT IS JUST A GAME TO HER. IF THEY TOLD PO WHO SHE IS, WITH THE S.I.C. DEAD, MAYBE SHE IS JUST GOING ON WHAT SHE WAS TOLD. AS OPHELIA'S DESCENDANT THIS IS PO'S HOUSE. MAYBE THAT IS WHY SHE IS ABOUT.

MY HOUSE?

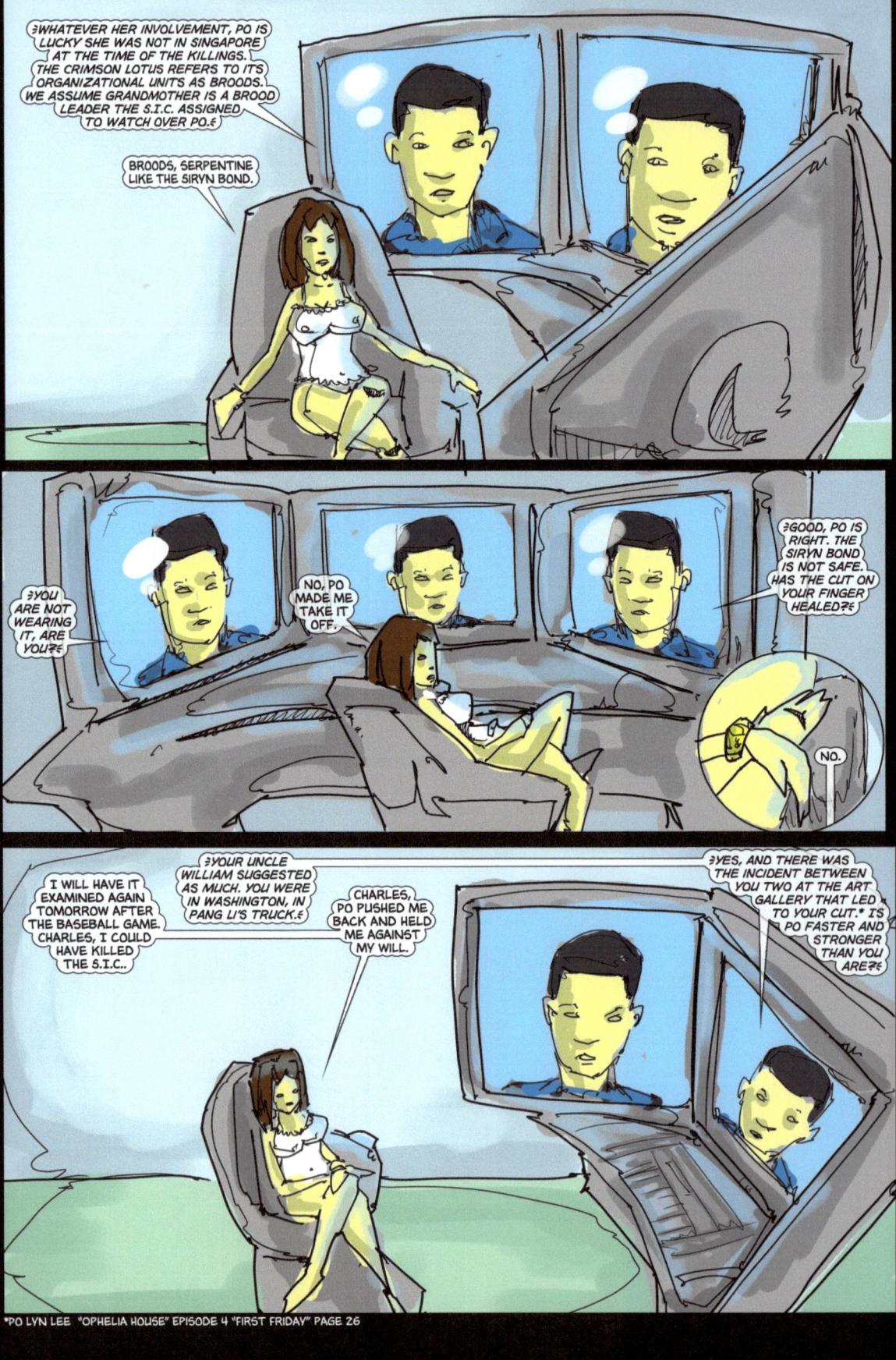

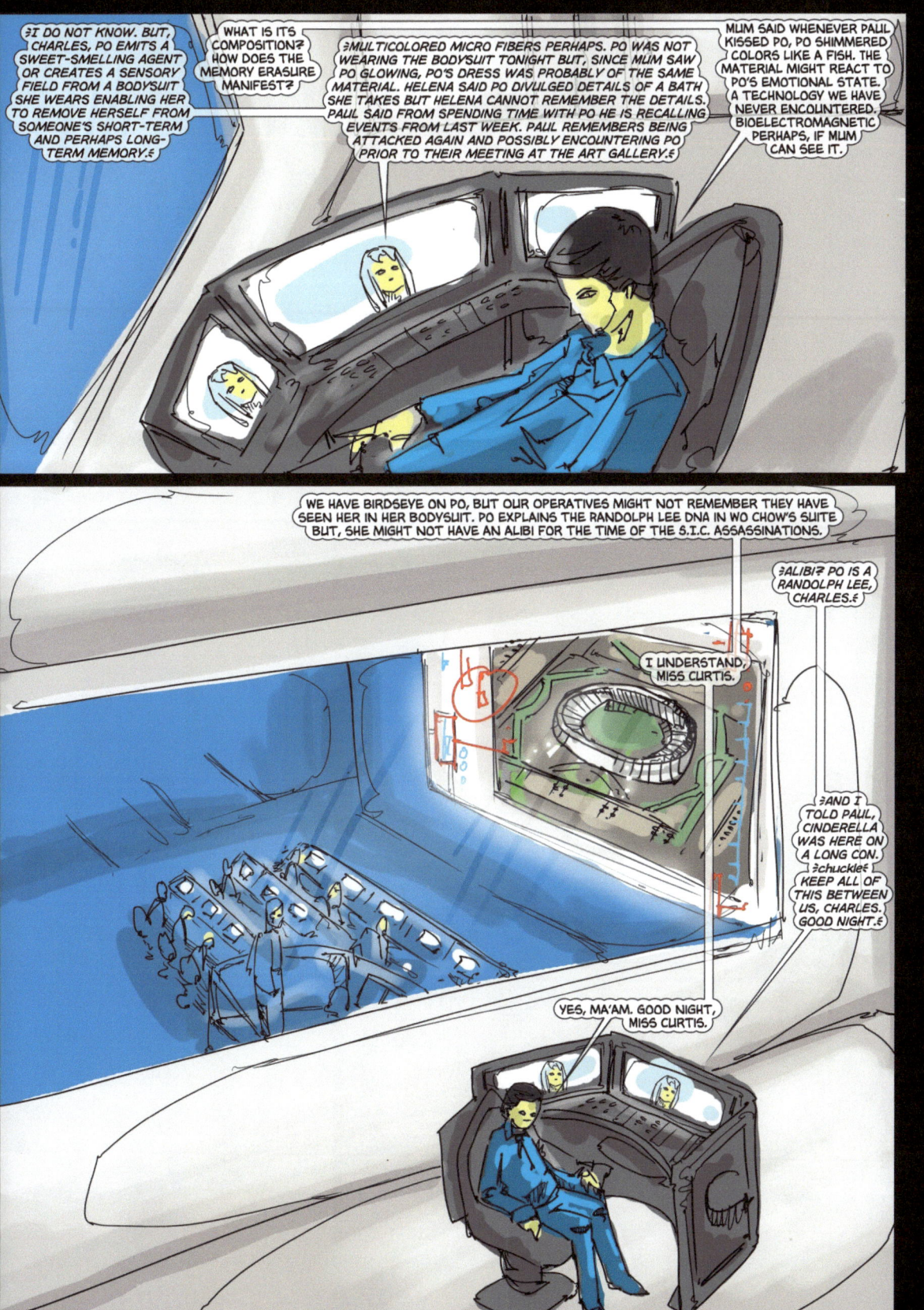

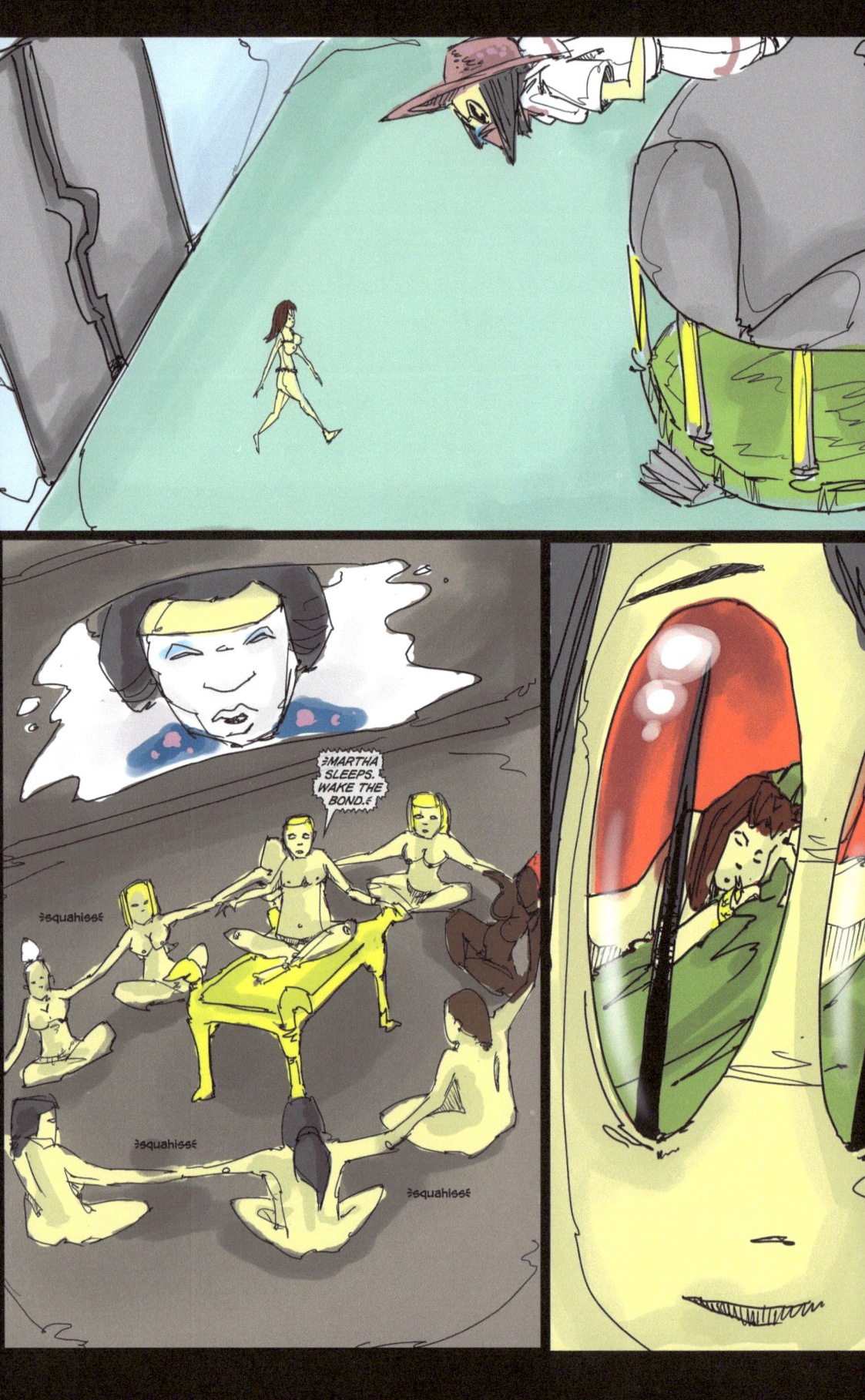

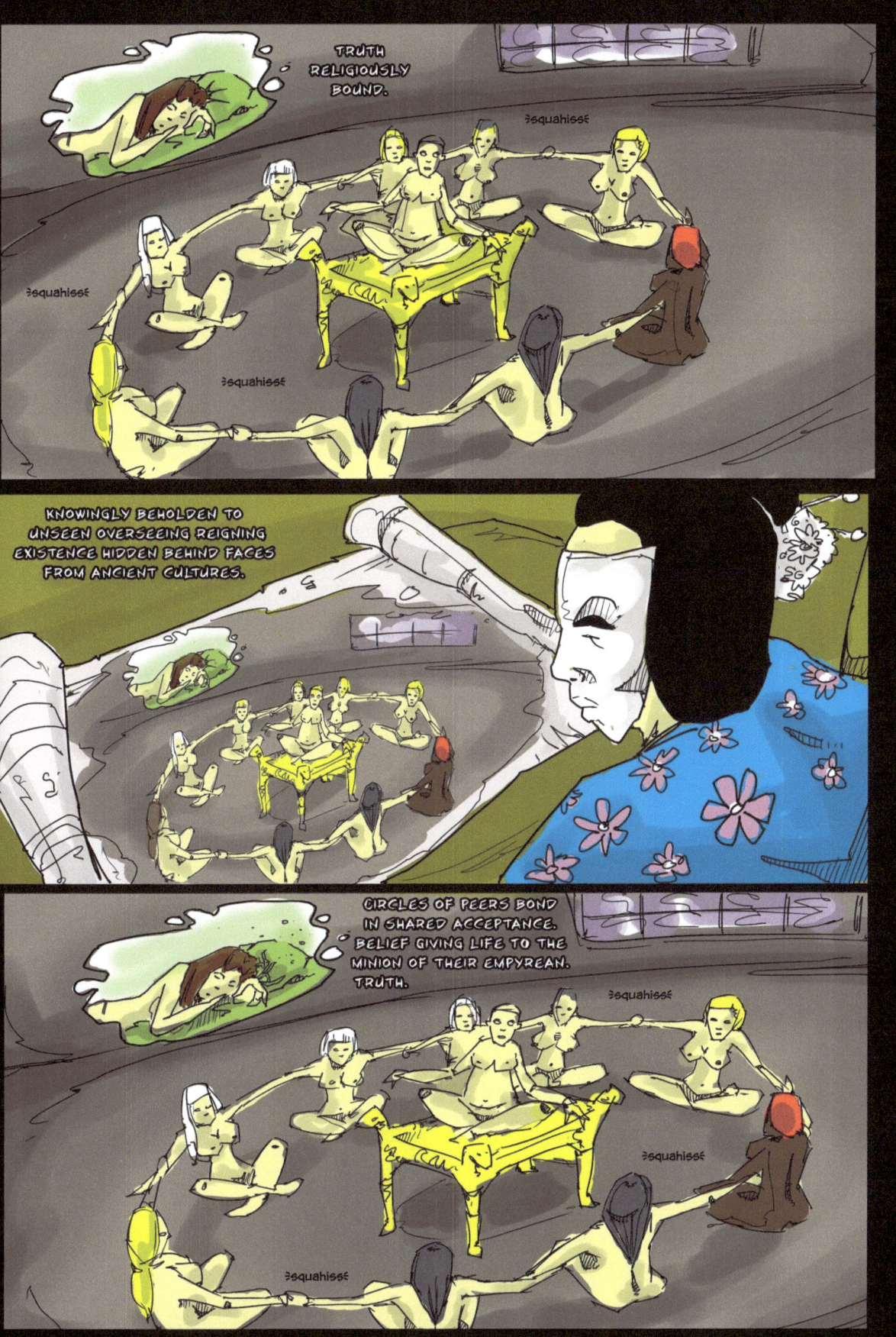

TRUTH RELIGIOUSLY BOUND.

≶squahiss≶

≶squahiss≶

≶squahiss≶

KNOWINGLY BEHOLDEN TO UNSEEN OVERSEEING REIGNING EXISTENCE HIDDEN BEHIND FACES FROM ANCIENT CULTURES.

CIRCLES OF PEERS BOND IN SHARED ACCEPTANCE. BELIEF GIVING LIFE TO THE MINION OF THEIR EMPYREAN. TRUTH.

≶squahiss≶

≶squahiss≶

≶squahiss≶

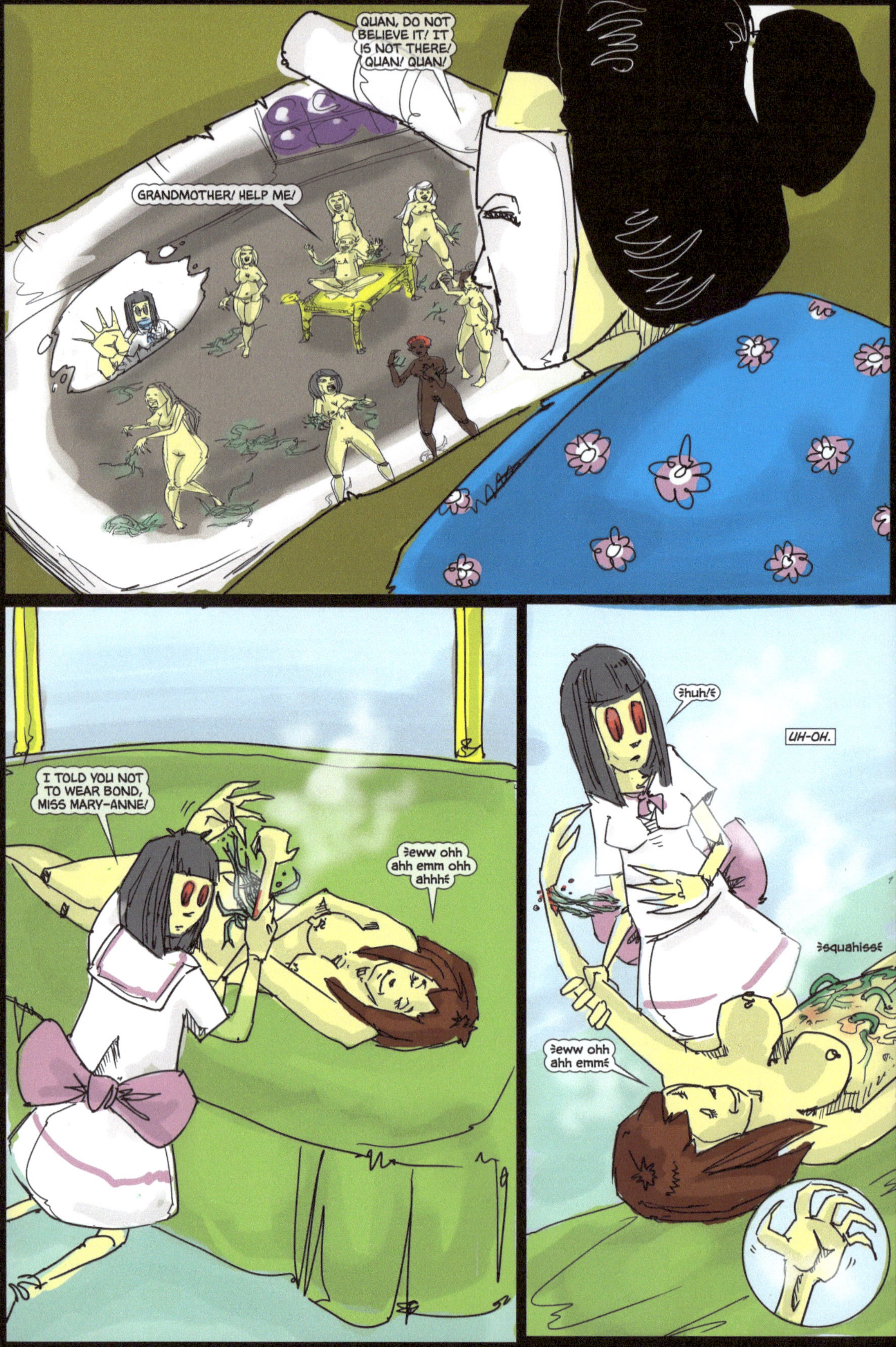

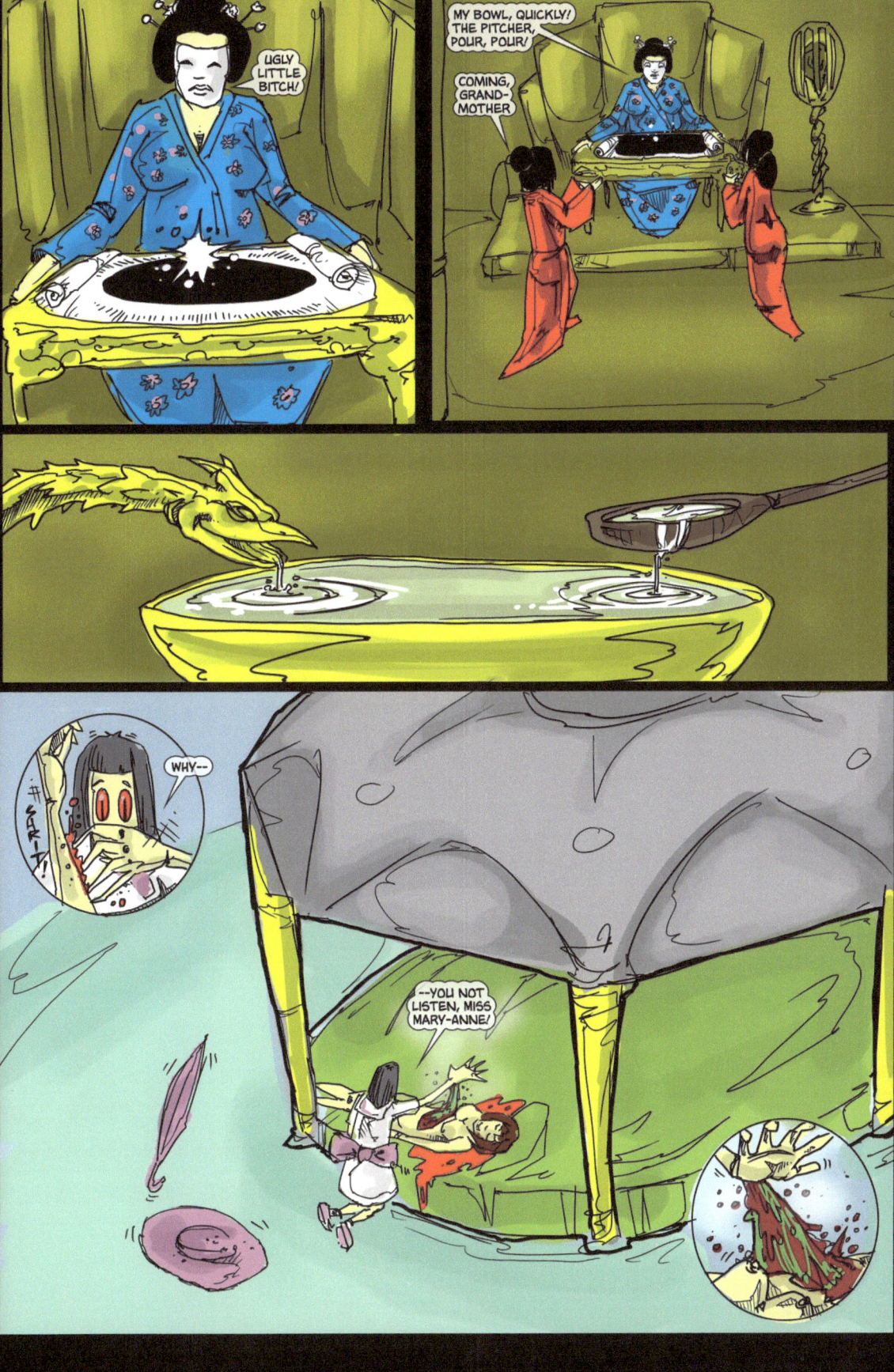

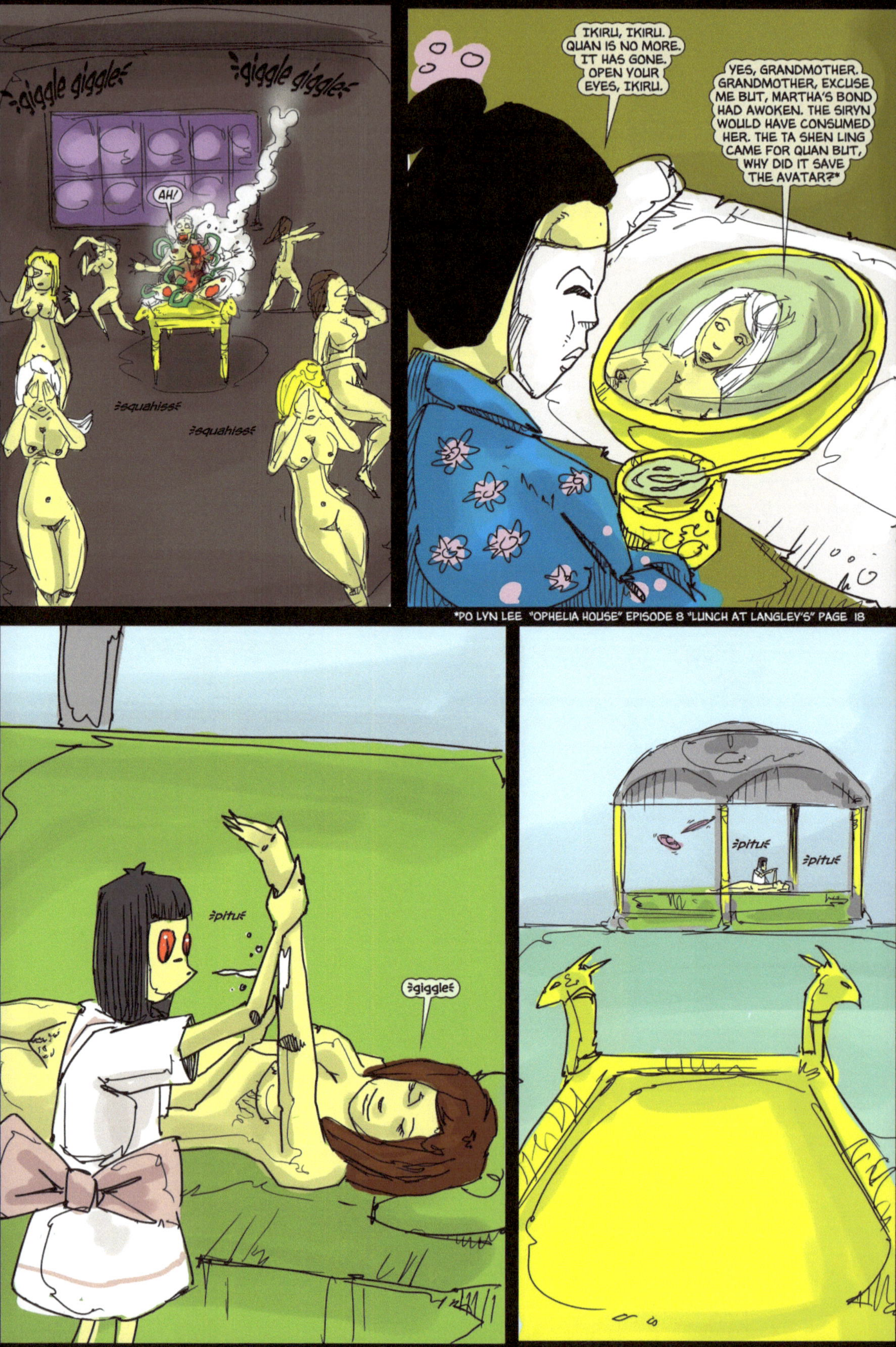

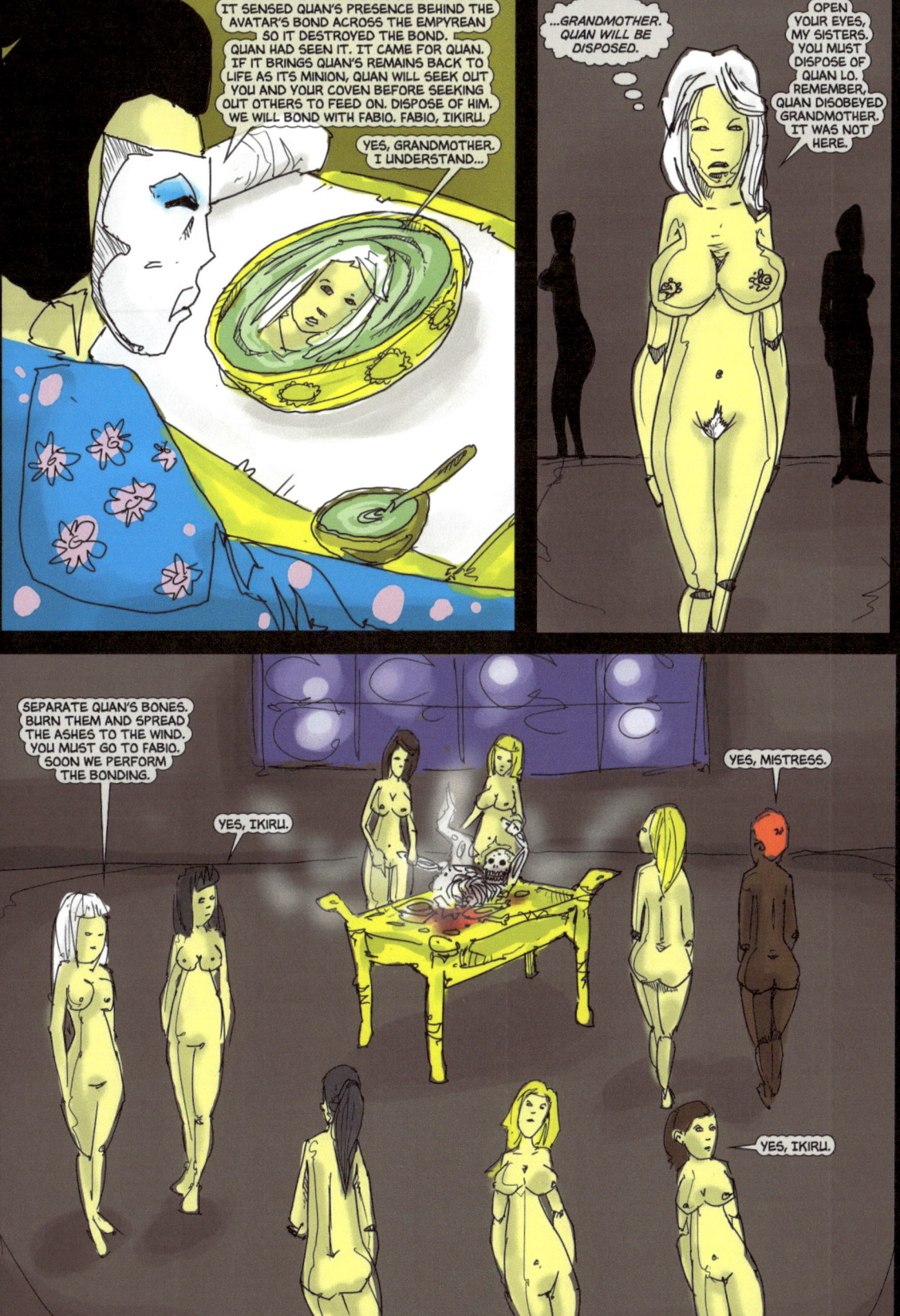

SISTER, SIN PANG!
NO HORSES ON THE DROME. WHOA.
≥huh!≤ WHOA, EASY.
SISTER, SIN PANG! SISTER, SIN PANG! YOUR KITE! IT CAME BACK!
LUCKY YOU.
SISTER, SIN PANG...BE CAREFUL!
NO WORRIES.

PO LYN LEE
OPHELIA HOUSE
NEXT ISSUE

"NO WORRIES"

"NO WORRIES"
DESTINY IS AT THE DOOR BUT LIZ IS JUST NOW DRESSING FOR THEIR DATE. SHE WILL BE LATE AND HELENA WORRIES ABOUT WHAT LADY LIBERTY TAKES TO THE BALL GAME. GRANDMOTHER HAS FRONT ROW SEATS TO EVERYTHING BUT THE E.A.I.C. BOARD IS IN THE DARK WITH THE MI CHU. MARTHA RANDOLPH CURTIS THE SECOND AND THE TA SHEN LING ARE IN THE MIX BUT MARY-ANNE DECIDES MR. RON HAND GLOVES CLASH WITH EVERYTHING. MI QUO TAKES AN E.A.I.C. CHARTED FLIGHT TO SLIDE SAFELY HOME TO HONG KONG.

CARLTON L. SAMPSON

POET, GRAPHIC NOVEL AUTHOR.
CARLTON@POLYNLEE.COM
OTHER WORK AVAILABLE AT:
WWW.PHASCISTCLOWNS.COM

ANDREW L. WILLIS

AKA, THIOBIS THE ARTIST
FINE ART, SCULPTURE, ANIMATION,
MUSIC, AND LITERARY.
ANDREW@POLYNLEE.COM
OTHER WORK AVAILABLE AT:
WWW.WAOOBAKEARTWORK.COM

STATION MANSION GARDENS
CARRIAGE HOUSE

DESTINY IS AT THE DOOR BUT LIZ IS JUST NOW DRESSING FOR THEIR DATE.
SHE WILL BE LATE AND HELENA WORRIES ABOUT WHAT LADY LIBERTY
TAKES TO THE BALL GAME. GRANDMOTHER HAS FRONT ROW SEATS TO
EVERYTHING BUT THE E.A.I.C. BOARD IS IN THE DARK WITH THE MI CHU.
MARTHA RANDOLPH CURTIS THE SECOND AND THE TA SHEN LING ARE IN
THE MIX BUT MARY-ANNE DECIDES MR. RON HAND GLOVES CLASH WITH
EVERYTHING. MI QUO TAKES AN E.A.I.C. CHARTED FLIGHT TO SLIDE SAFELY
HOME TO HONG KONG.

NEXT ISSUE

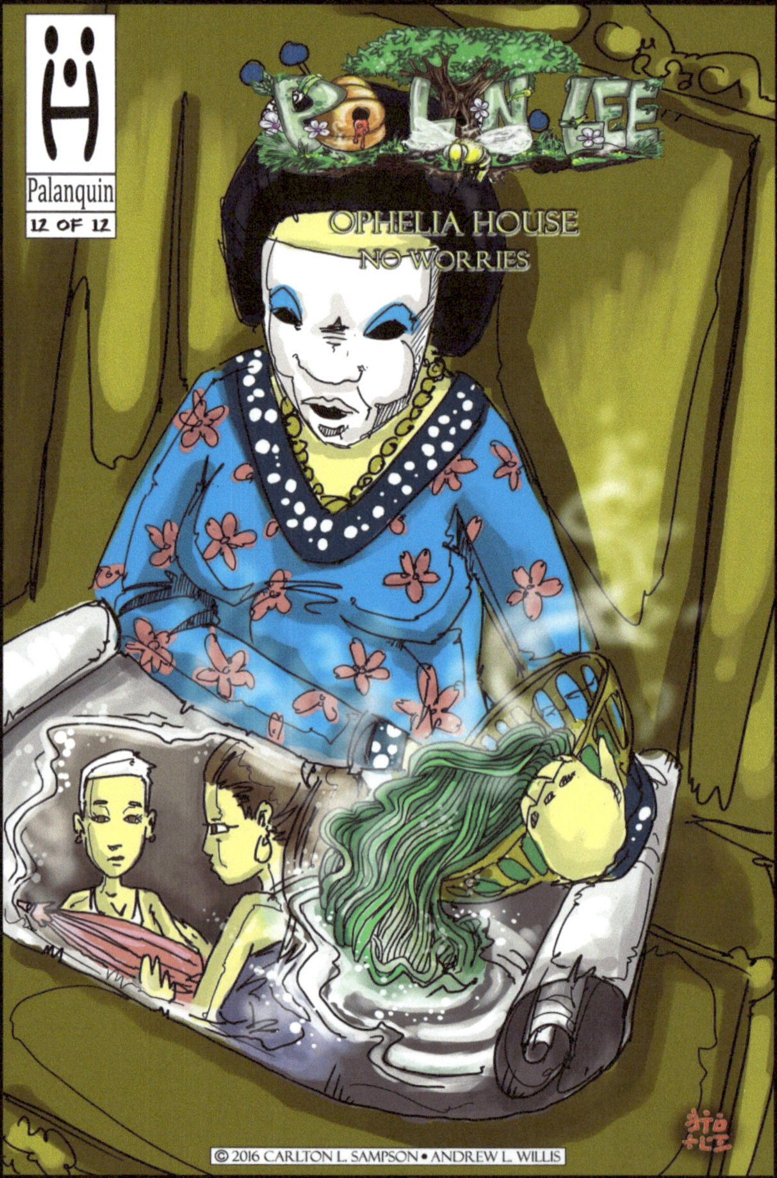

 WWW.POLYNLEE.COM

www.ingramcontent.com/pod-product-compliance
Lightning Source LLC
Chambersburg PA
CBHW041537240626

47164CB00002B/42